SAM & UNCLE JOE
LEARNING TO SERVE AND PROTECT.

Written by: Phoebe London

D1293656

Sam & Uncle Joe: Learning to serve and protect © 2022

All rights reserved.
Phoebe London and Jos. B own all rights to text and illustrations.

©2022 Phoebe London and Jos. B

Phoebe London is identified as the author and Schnappico Arts
is identified as the commissioned illustrator of the work.

Published by Phoebe London

No part of this book may be reproduced in any form or by any means
(electronic, mechanical, photocopying, recording or any other type)
without prior written permission of the author except for use in book reviews or brief quotations.

To all children remember,
you are a promise

Sam dashed out of his bed with a big grin on his face!
It's Saturday, and His favorite Uncle Joe is coming for a visit.
Hooray! With the sun beaming brightly in the morning sky,
Sam is all geared up to spend his day with Uncle Joe.

Uncle Joe always comes with lots of Double Choco ice cream,
which is Sam's favorite. They would play all day and spend
the evening having ice cream. Sam would listen to Uncle Joe's
war stories from serving in the military and law enforcement
which was Sam's favorite part. Sam was always ready
to listen to Uncle Joe's war stories.

"Slow down,"
Mama said as Sam gulped another spoonful of cereal down his throat. "You will get hiccups if you rush your food like that. Why the rush? "Asked Mama.

"I'm going to Ken's house to get my video game before Uncle Joe gets here. I wouldn't want to keep him waiting," replied Sam, with his mouth full of cereal.

Sam skipped to Ken's house, singing along.
It was such a beautiful day, and Sam's smile was as bright as the sun. He skipped to the end of the street until he reached house number 10, where Ken lived with his siblings and grandma.
He knocked and waited for someone to answer.
Ken's sister, Fiona, answered the door.
"Hi Fiona, is Ken around?" he asked her.
Immediately, Ken came outside.
'Yo, Sam! What's up with you?' he asked.
"I came for my video game," Sam replied.
"Oh! Sure," Come on in," said Ken, taking Sam to his room.

Sam walked with Ken to his room,
where he gave him his video game.

"My grandma is making breakfast.
Do you care to join us?" Ken asked.

"No, thanks, I've already had mine, which I finished in five bites,"
said Sam, grinning at Ken.

"Also, Uncle Joe is visiting today!
I don't want to keep him waiting. Bye!"
Sam said as he left for his house.

On his way home, Sam saw a group of kids fighting. "Order!" someone shouted.

He struggled to hear what the person said but could not make it out. He was very shocked to see a teenager pointing a gun at Ken's brother, Adolf.

Sam tried to scream, but to no avail, and became terrified with his mouth drying fast. Sam watched wide-eyed as the teenager pulled the trigger, shot Adolf twice in the chest, and as Adolf fell to the ground, the teenager ran away with the gun.

Sam opened his mouth to scream again, but all that came out was a low 'ah.'

"Someone has been shot. Call an ambulance!"
Sam heard someone else shout in the distance. Neighbors came out; They called an ambulance to take Adolf to the hospital, but they confirmed Adolf dead before the ambulance could get to the hospital.

A police officer who arrived at the scene took
Sam back to his house.

"Oh, my darling boy!" exclaimed Mama and pulled him
into her embrace.

"What happened?" Mama asked the police as she took Sam's
hand and held him close to her.

"There was a shooting," the police officer explained.

"Oh, no!" she cried out. "Was someone hurt?"

"Yes, young Adolf was killed. We will investigate the crime. I have
to get to the station now," the police officer answered politely.

"Be safe. Keep your eyes open for any strange people or noises
and call the police immediately," said the police officer before
leaving.

Mama thanked the officer. Then she took Sam into the house
and hugged him closely. "It is all right, Sam; you are home now.
Dad and Mama will make sure you are safe," she said to him.

Sam was so traumatized that he couldn't speak.
He could not stop thinking about Adolf. The sound of the gunshot
played in his head repeatedly like a nightmare.

He wished his dad would come home from work.
Sam cried bitterly as he threw several punches at his pillow;
he did not realize Uncle Joe had finally come.

"How is my big boy doing?"
Uncle Joe asked at the entrance to his room.
Sam looked up, startled at Uncle Joe's voice,
and ran to hug him with his face covered in tears.

"What's wrong?" Uncle Joe asked him.

Sam broke out in a sob, unable to reply.

"He saw his friend's brother get shot today,"
Sam's Mama said from behind Uncle Joe.

Uncle Joe held him close.
"It is okay, Sam,"
he said as he lifted Sam into his arms.

"Look how big you've grown,"
he said. They both went out to sit on the porch.

"See, I have guns too, but they never draw blood from people.
The green one shoots water," Sam said sadly, his voice breaking.

"My dear Sam," Uncle Joe said softly, "there are different guns.
There is a toy gun that children like you play with. You use it to
pretend to shoot people. You may use this one anytime because it
does not hurt anyone. Then there is another type, which is not a
toy gun. This gun can harm people or damage an organ
permanently. That is the gun you saw today, Sam. It is not the
type of gun that you play with."

"It is very wrong to hurt or harm someone else. It would be best if
you did not handle a real gun. You are a child and do not know
how to hold or control a real gun without hurting yourself or other
people," Uncle Joe explained.

"Why did Adolf get shot?" Sam asked. "Adolf was a good person. He helped all the kids in the neighborhood," Sam said with tears in his eyes.

"Listen, Sam," Uncle Joe said, "We know that there are a lot of problems kids have to experience these days. It is not always easy to be a kid. It is not clear why people do the things they do, but we can choose how we serve and protect each other and ourselves."

"I'm so sorry that you had to see what happened to Adolf today," Mama said.

"I'm scared," said Sam, trembling. Uncle Joe hugged him. "Nothing will happen to you. I'm here, and so are your parents; they will protect you even when I am gone. Okay?" Sam nodded in agreement. "Have you forgotten who I am?" Uncle Joe asked him teasingly. Sam nodded again.

"My uncle, you are the Great Lieutenant Colonel of the United States Army!" Sam replied, smiling.

"Be strong like your uncle, okay?" His Mama said with a smile.

Mama, is it okay if I make some cookies for Ken and his sister?"
Sam asked, his voice now full of concern;

"I know they will need a friend. I want to help them,
just as Uncle Joe said"

"Of course, you can, Sam!" Mama replied.
"That is very thoughtful of you. Sending some homemade snacks
is such a pleasant way of serving others. I am sure they would be
happy, knowing you are there for them during this hard time."

Later that evening, Sam went over to Ken's house with Uncle Joe. There were other kids from the neighborhood too.
All the kids were seated on the floor with sorrowful faces.
Uncle Joe looked around the room and saw a piano set. He went and sat down and started to play some notes, singing along.
All the kids began to listen, and the gloomy atmosphere in the living room became a little lighter.

"This was my favorite song when I was a kid,"
Uncle Joe told the kids with a smile after landing on the last key.

"I am a promise; I am a possibility; I am for a purpose with a capital letter P; I can be anything I want to be."

"I like it too," Sara said with a sheepish smile.

"Sam made some cookies for everyone to enjoy,"
Uncle Joe said as he took one for himself.
"I know you kids don't know me. I'm a retired Lieutenant
Colonel of the US army," he said. "I am Sam's uncle.
My name is Joe; you can call me Uncle Joe.
You don't have to be afraid."
"Someone killed Adolf. He was like a big brother to all of us.
He always used to look out for us," Maria, one kid, said.
"He used to protect me from bullies at school," Tim said.
"I know, you must feel sad," Uncle Joe said.
"We cannot change what happened to Adolf, but we can try to
prevent something like this from happening again.
We must learn to serve and protect others and ourselves."
With passion, he pumped his clenched fist in the air.
"How?" asked Ken, with his brows furrowed together.
"By taking care of ourselves and those around us, we cannot
control what other people do, but we can control our behaviors.
Killing or hurting people is bad; you should not speak rudely to
other people, and you should be nice to each other.
Because we never know what problems the other person
could be dealing with. We should always be kind."
"That way, the world will be a safer and happier place for us all,"
Sam said.

"Yes! That is right, Sam," said Uncle Joe, giving Sam a nod. "You all can make your community and the world a better place. I want you to know that you are not alone. Your family will do everything they can do to protect you and keep you safe," Uncle Joe said.

"That is what my dad also told me," Maria said.

"Good! Now let me tell you a little story that I hope will inspire, educate and motivate you all."

All the kids were listening intensely to Uncle Joe as he unveiled the story. "Once, during my military days, we were still on the battlefield. They assigned My Team and I on a mission." He started. It was to defend our great country. God bless America."

"God bless the Nation," chorused the Kids.

That's the spirit of enthusiasm! Guess what the goal of the mission was. "What?" all the kids said in unison, craving to know.

"Our goal was to save the people captured by a dangerous terrorist group and rescue them. They dispatched our team in the air; we saved many lives and many children, just like you,we took them out of harm's way.

"Kids, in whatever situations you find yourself, I want you always to remember this; there are ways to survive. Imagine an armed robber robs the mall you are shopping in? Or you see someone in danger. How can you save the victim? Or let's say they kidnapped you. How will you handle the situation?

All the kids were listening intently, very focused on Uncle Joe.

"Now listen closely; in a situation like a robbery, if you hear shots being fired, lie low, or hide behind a concrete wall or something solid in order to avoid flying objects. Also, when you need to rescue someone or find people in danger, the first thing you do is look around for a comfort zone, take them there, cheer them up, and call for help as soon as you can. If someone has physically hurt them, attend to them with first aid treatment."

"Don't get kidnapped! But in such cases, also make sure you cooperate with the kidnapper, follow their orders, be brave and confident, and don't act funny by trying to escape. Wait until you are rescued; only then will you be safe."

"I hope you will find these tips useful in times of trouble." He finished and gave the kids a wink.
"Roger that, sir!" replied all the kids with enthusiasm.
"The Police are not good, and they are not doing their job well!" Patrick shouted.
Uncle Joe looked at him, and then he replied gently,
"Yes, police can be bad, but there are many outstanding police officers, too. And they are doing their best to make sure that people are not hurt. That's their job.

"Now I want you all to remember three important things about serving and protecting others," said Uncle Joe, holding up three fingers.

"Number one, you have to be aware of your surroundings at all times. Stay alert, and if you suspect anything unusual, tell an adult whom you trust immediately.

Number two, if you find yourself threatened, try not to panic; instead, get yourself to safety as soon as possible. And Number three, if you see someone engaging in something wrong or dangerous, do not involve yourself and don't call them out for it."

'If none of you join any dangerous groups or gangs or involve yourselves with violence, what do you think will happen?' Uncle Joe asked them.

'Everywhere will be safe for everyone,' Sam yelled.

'That is right, Sam! You all make your community and the world a better place and a safer place. I want you to know that you are not alone. Your family and community will do everything they can do to protect you and make sure nothing bad happens to you,' Uncle Joe said.

'Good! Another thing, take your education seriously, stay in school, and listen to your teachers. Learn to be compassionate and kind towards each other. You protect me; I protect you. You got my back; I got your back. You have a friend in me, and I have a friend in you. We all have friends in each other.'

He ended and spread out his arms for a hug. All the kids rushed into his arms in a tight embrace.

"Together, we shall be strong! Together we shall make a difference! Together we shall serve and protect!" He affirmed. They were no longer sad and scared.

Instead, they believed that together, they were stronger, they would make a difference, they would learn to serve and protect each other.

THE END

Made in the USA
Coppell, TX
09 April 2022

76228679R00024